'Mum said we have to wait in the car,' bossed Eppie. 'And if we get out of the car and start being naughty she said she'll be so absolutely furious that even the ants in our pants will run away.'

'I'll give you a million dollars if you come and play with me,' Zeke persisted.

'Don't be dumb, Zeke,' said Eppie.

'All right, I'll give you ten million dollars.'

'Oh, OK,' said Eppie.

So Eppie started to climb out her window, and she was nearly through when her foot slipped on the door handle, and she fell straight out of the window and landed head first on the road, in that very same pothole, with just her legs and her feet poking out.

**Also available by
Gretel Killeen in Red Fox**

My Sister's an Alien

My Sister's a
Yo-yo

MY SISTER'S A YO-YO
A RED FOX BOOK 0 09 943368 0

Published in Great Britain by Red Fox,
an imprint of Random House Children's Books

PRINTING HISTORY
First published in Australia by Random House Australia Pty Ltd, 1997
Red Fox edition published, 2002

1 3 5 7 9 10 8 6 4 2

Copyright © Gretel Killeen, 1997
Illustrations copyright © Leigh Hobbs, 1997

Papers used by Random House Children's Books are natural, recyclable products made
from wood grown in sustainable forests. The manufacturing processes conform to the
environmental regulations of the country of origin.

Set in 17/21pt Bembo Schoolbook
Red Fox books are published by Random House Children's Books,
61-63 Uxbridge Road, London W5 5SA,
a division of The Random House Group Ltd,
in Australia by Random House Australia (Pty) Ltd,
20 Alfred Street, Milsons Point, Sydney, NSW 2061, Australia,
in New Zealand by Random House New Zealand Ltd,
18 Poland Road, Glenfield, Auckland 10, New Zealand,
and in South Africa by Random House (Pty) Ltd,
Endulini, 5A Jubilee Road, Parktown 2193, South Africa

THE RANDOM HOUSE GROUP Limited Reg. No. 954009

A CIP catalogue record for this book is available from the British Library.

Printed and bound in Great Britain by Bookmarque Ltd, Croydon, Surrey

www.kidsatrandomhouse.co.uk

GRETEL KILLEEN

My Sister's a
Yo - yo

Illustrated by Leigh Hobbs

RED FOX

A message from your author...

WARNING: DO NOT BE AFRAID, LAUGH RUDELY OR BURP WITH SURPRISE.

In Australia we speak English just like you do but occasionally we use completely different words. For example, we don't say **trousers**, we say **pants**; we don't say **crisps**, we say **chips**; and we don't say **person from England**, we say **Pommie**.

Some of our Aussie words have been changed in this book so that you **Pommies** can understand them, but some of them haven't. So just in case you're wondering what on earth those words mean let me tell you that a **texta** is a coloured felt-tipped pen, a **milkbar** is a place to buy milk and hamburgers and lollies, and a **slippery dip** is a slide.

Now start reading and I hope you love this book so much you want to eat it.

P.S. We don't recommend that you eat this book.

It's not often that the entire universe explodes into smithereens and splatters cows and gizzards and bananas and ears all over the galaxy . . . and it wasn't happening today either.

Zeke was bored. He'd been sitting in the car for a dillion years waiting for his mother to find her glasses.

She'd put them down inside the house somewhere and she was searching high and low – but if you can't see a thing when you're not wearing your glasses, how are you ever going to find them?

So Zeke was waiting for his mother to drive him to school, but at this rate she'd be driving him to university.

Zeke had absolutely nothing to do.

His mother had said, 'Don't get out of the car,' so he was sitting there with nothing to do.

Slowly he wound the window down, and then he wound it up. Then he wound it down again, paused, and wound it up once more.

He pretended to get his hand stuck in the window, then he picked his nose and ate the snot.

Then he pretended the car was a spaceship and he was flying to his very own powerful planet where the only things anyone did all day long were watch television, drink Coke and not clean their teeth.

Then he got bored again, so he did a little fart, and then he imagined that all the air had gone from the car and he was dying of suffocation (this actually wasn't very hard), and then he stopped and burped the alphabet.

Then he breathed out deeply, rolled his eyes and checked under the car seats for jewelled boxes of hidden treasure, and that's where he found his favourite thing in the world.

That's where he found his yo-yo.
Zeke sat and held his yo-yo for a while.

And then he got bored.

Then he wound the window down again, leaned outside the car and played with the yo-yo.

He spun the yo-yo as far as he could and it came back faster than a speeding bullet and donked him on the head.

Then he fell out of the car. And landed in a pothole.

Zeke sat dazed in the pothole for a while but then he got worried about his mum finding him so he imagined that he was Superman (or some other superhero who didn't actually wear blue tights with undies over the outside) and used every rippling muscle in his awesome body to climb out of the treacherous chasm.

When he'd finished, he got dizzy
again, crawled off the road and sat down
on the footpath.

He just sat, sat, sat . . . and then of
course he got bored again.

And that's when he spied his sister, Eppie.

Eppie was in the front seat of the car
staring at him. She'd actually been sitting
in the car the whole time but Zeke never
paid her much attention because he
didn't think she was very important. In
fact Zeke and his friends believed that all
girls were unimportant and useless for just
about everything. But there was one
thing that Eppie was the best in the world
for . . . and that was being teased. (Ah yes,
'teasing': an ancient and excellent form
of entertainment for brothers and sisters
of all ages.)

'Hey, Eppie, want to catch my yo-yo?'
Zeke yelled.

'Mum said we have to wait in the car,'

bossed Eppie. 'And if we get out of the car and start being naughty she said she'll be so absolutely furious that even the ants in our pants will run away.'

'I'll give you a million dollars if you come and play with me,' Zeke persisted.

'Don't be dumb, Zeke,' said Eppie.

'All right, I'll give you ten million dollars.'

'Oh, OK,' said Eppie.

So Eppie started to climb out her window, and she was nearly through when her foot slipped on the door handle, and she fell straight out of the window and landed head first on the road, in that very same pothole, with just her legs and her feet poking out.

Zeke thought Eppie looked the best he'd ever seen her until moments later a truck carrying a house ran right over the top of her and squished Eppie to the size of a strawberry.

Well Zeke took one quick look at his shrunken, upside-down, strawberry-sized sister and said, 'Mum's going to explode.' Then, before Eppie had a chance to even begin to cry, Zeke took a very deep breath and said, 'I suggest we make the most of our remaining minutes of freedom and try to have some fun before Mum comes out and kills us. What do you reckon?'

Eppie immediately agreed with Zeke (but that's because she didn't have a clue what he was talking about).

'OK, Eppie. Stand right there, and let the games begin,' said Zeke as he looped his finger into the yo-yo string and then swung the yo-yo as hard as he could towards his little sister. But just when Eppie was about to catch the yo-yo, Zeke suddenly tugged as hard as he could on the string, and pulled the yo-yo away.

He laughed at Eppie of course, because she looked so silly grabbing at the air, and Eppie pretended to sulk of course, and then she said she didn't want to play any more of course, and that she was going to tell Mum that Zeke had got out of the car.

'And what are you going to say happened to you?' Zeke demanded, looking straight at his berry-sized sister.

Eppie started to sob, great big little-girl sopping wet tears (not little little-girl sopping wet tears), and each tear was nearly as big as her head, and Zeke was worried that Eppie would drown in the flood and then he'd have no one to tease.

And so he said in his nicest voice, which he only used when he really wanted something, 'I'm really sorry for laughing at you, Eppie. I promise I won't do it again.'

And Eppie was bored so she said, 'Oh, OK.'

'Now this time just stand there, and we'll see if you blink,' Zeke said as he whirled his yo-yo right near Eppie's face. But Eppie blinked, and Zeke called her a scaredy cat, and then he got bored again, and she got bored again too. They were going to pick a fight in fact, just for something to do, but instead Zeke said, 'I've got an idea: I'll whirl the yo-yo on your head!'

Their mum was nowhere to be seen.

She could have been sucked up by the vacuum cleaner.

She could have been swallowed by the sink.

She could have been eaten by the goldfish, or she could have blindly locked herself in the broom cupboard, thinking that she'd found the front door.

Whatever the case, Mum wasn't nearby, so Eppie agreed to let her brother whirl his yo-yo on her head.

So Zeke stood over tiny Eppie and took very careful aim, then he gently dropped his yo-yo down the string, and whirled it on Eppie's head.

And Eppie laughed, and Zeke laughed, and so they did it again.

Faster.

And they laughed.

And so they did it again.

Faster.

And they laughed.

And so they did it again.

Faster.

And they laughed.

And so they did it again and again, and they laughed until they thought they would split, and they did it again, one more time, faster and faster and faster and faster, and that's when they heard their mother finally coming out of the house.

'Aaaaaaagh!' screamed Eppie.

'Aaaaaaagh!' screamed Zeke.

'Get back in the car!' they both
screamed.

Eppie went to run one way and Zeke
went to run the other, but they only
made it a few steps each before
something suddenly stopped them.

Was it the hidden force of evil, or maybe guilt or fear? Or was it perhaps some invisible alien attempting to kidnap them for a rather huge ransom that their mother would probably never pay because it would 'only encourage them'?

Or was it something far more boring?

Well yes it was something incredibly boring, too boring really to mention. It was Eppie's hair tangled up in Zeke's yo-yo – but there was definitely no time to get her off.

Their mother was coming, they were going to get caught, they had to think quickly or else. Mum had said, 'Don't get out of the car,' but get out of the car's what they'd done. And not only that but Eppie had shrunk and her hair was an absolute mess.

They could hear the clip-clop of Mum's heels on the drive. They could almost feel her breath. In just a few moments their lives would be over, with probably no TV for a week!

'Think,' thought Zeke. 'Think,' thought Eppie. 'Think, think, think, think, think.'

Suddenly Zeke had an idea and quick as a flash he wound up his yo-yo and Eppie as well, shoved the whole lot into his school bag and started to sing *I Will Always Love You,* that all-time classic by Whitney Houston.

'Ah, my favourite song,' hummed Mum as she fumbled her way out to the car.

'Have you seen my glasses?' Mum
said to the tree, and sat in the back seat
of the car. 'Where's the steering wheel
gone?' she continued to say before
moving to the front seat to drive.

Anyway Eppie and Zeke didn't get
caught, and Mum drove them to school
wailing like a police siren to warn
people that she was approaching. When

they finally got to school Mum said,
'Have a nice day, try hard, be good,
concentrate, eat your lunch, have fun,
blah blah blah, I'll pick you up at half
past three. Bye, Zeke.'

'Bye, Mum.'

'Bye, Eppie.'

'Bye, Mum.'

Mum continued to look for her
glasses and kissed the car seat goodbye.

Meanwhile Zeke clambered out of the car with little Eppie in his school bag. By this time Mum had found her glasses on top of her head, but Zeke and Eppie had already gone into school.

In the playground Zeke stood wondering what to do. He had a sister the size of a nose attached to his favourite toy and stuffed in the bottom of his school bag.

Life was not looking good, especially when Joel Slime grabbed Zeke's school bag for a joke and threw it way up in a tree, and the strap got caught on a high

pointy branch, and Eppie just hung
there, in the bag, swaying in the breeze
until Zeke took a pot shot with a rock,
and Eppie and the bag and the yo-yo
and the string fell back down to earth –
with a thump.

Clang! rang the school bell.

Zeke was worried about his sister (but only because she might have splattered all over his lunch and he liked to eat enormous amounts and he didn't have any money for the tuck-shop and he couldn't possibly die of starvation today because he was wearing embarrassing undies). So as all the kids filed off to class, Zeke ran to the toilets as fast as he could, opened the zipper of his bag and searched inside for Eppie.

The first thing he found was that his whole lunch was squashed and squished all through his bag, and the second thing he found was that Eppie was squashed and squished all through his bag as well.

Strawberry-sized Eppie looked like fruit salad as she sat there all covered in banana.

She may have looked all cute and
funny but Eppie was in a really bad
mood. Zeke tried to pick her up
veeeeeeeeeeery carefully, but she bit
him hard on the finger and Zeke got
such a huge surprise that he dropped
Eppie down the toilet. PLOP!

'Glet mle blout,' Eppie gargled.

'Not till you say sorry for biting my
finger!' Zeke yelled down into the toilet
bowl.

'Get me out,' yelled Eppie, 'or I'll scream and scream and scream and scream until you go deaf and blind with shock and vultures come and nibble your eyeballs.'

'Oh all right, be quiet,' said Zeke.

So then Zeke got two strong sticks from the playground and used them like chopsticks to lift his sopping-wet sister from inside the loo.

After she came up gasping and spluttering, Zeke turned the basin tap on ever so gently and stuck Eppie and the yo-yo under the cold running water. They were nearly clean when he applied the soap for added shine and Eppie became as slippery as a slug, slipped through his fingers, whirled round the basin and nearly went down the plughole.

But Zeke grabbed her as quick as a flash and actually saved her life. (He'll

never forget this of course, and will
mention it once a day for the rest of his
life, and twice a day at Easter when
he'll want some of Eppie's chocolate
eggs.) Then he dried Eppie under the
hot-air drier and put her in his pocket,
blew his nose on some toilet paper, stuck
that in his pocket too, and went to class.

On the way to his classroom Zeke got bored again (unbelievable I know, but some people do bore very easily). So he pulled the plaster off his elbow and put it in his pocket, on top of the toilet paper and on top of Eppie too. Then he pulled the scab from his sore elbow and put that in his pocket as well.

When Zeke got to the classroom he sat down at his desk, found the chewing gum he'd stuck under his chair yesterday, and started to give it a chew. But before he'd even had a chance to make the chewing gum all soft again, his teacher, super-skinny Miss Snailheadface, called out from behind her desk, 'What are you chewing, Zeke?'

'Oh nothing,' he replied.

'Well get that "nothing" out of my sight, and put it away in your pocket.'

So Zeke took the chewing gum out of his mouth and stuck that in his pocket

too, right on Eppie's nose, and then the school morning began.

For most of the subjects Eppie sat quietly in the bottom of Zeke's pocket. Then during maths she fell asleep, and during spelling she snored. And then during music class she danced and sang and no matter what Zeke did to shut her up she just would not stop. He tried to plonk her on the head with his pencil rubber. He tried squeezing her still with his fingers. He tried offering his sister a magic castle in the clouds. But Eppie just would not stop.

(It would have been all right if she'd been a gentle dancer and a quiet singer but Eppie danced like a milkshake maker and sang like a half-dead cat.)

Miss Snailheadface asked, 'Who is making that noise?'

And some loud-mouthed kid bellowed, 'It's Zeke who's making all the noise, and check out his pocket. It's dancing!'

Zeke could feel the eyes on him. He had to do something quick smart, so he rose from his chair and started to dance and sing like an opera singer with excited fleas in his navel.

Well Miss Snailheadface took one long look at Zeke dancing like a mad boy in the middle of the class and singing like a fighter jet plummeting to earth, and she sent him off to see Nurse Chunkus, who worked in the school sick bay.

('Excellent,' thought Zeke. 'Now I'll have the time and space to undo Eppie, stretch her back to shape, send her back to her class, and then play with my yo-yo.')

Zeke stood up to go to the sick bay, pretending that he was disappointed and ill, and walked across the room like the dribble from a spilt milkshake. Then, as soon as he'd stepped out the door, he skipped all the way up to the sick bay. He was happy and free and full of joy, until the bell went for recess.

Boring.

So every other kid in the whole universe ran out to play and Zeke had to sit there, waiting for Nurse Chunkus, having absolutely no fun whatsoever – and all because of Eppie.

'Well then,' said Nurse Chunkus, when she finally entered the room with a moustache of cream and icing sugar. 'What seems to be the problem? I understand you have a jiggling lump in your side and there's something wrong with your voice. Well, first things first: the lump.'

Nurse Chunkus made Zeke stand up and turn round and she said, 'Oh yes, my goodness, look at that! You'd better take your shorts off, Zeke, and let me get a closer look.'

'Take my shorts off!' thought Zeke. 'I would rather be eaten alive by a golden cockroach than show this woman my bum.' And then, like a miracle, the telephone rang, and the nurse left the room to answer it.

With Eppie in his pocket Zeke stood wondering whether or not he should take his shorts off, or just run as fast as he could to the hills of Transylvania where he could grow a horrible wiry beard, wear a silly hat, live like a hermit for the rest of his life and never ever get caught.

Escape sounded like the best option but Nurse Chunkus was talking on the phone by the front doorway and there was obviously no easy way out, so Zeke looked like he'd have, like he'd have to, like he'd have . . . to . . . of course, take Eppie out of his left-hand pocket and put her in the right one instead. And so he did exactly that and then the nurse came back.

'Well, Zeke, I told you to show me the lump,' she said.

'There's no need to now,' Zeke replied, 'because as you can see, the lump's completely gone. So can I go out and play?'

And Nurse said, 'This is very odd. I'm sure it was there before,' and she put on her glasses, the really thick ones, and made Zeke turn in a circle slowly.

He felt like a ballerina inside a music box (he felt like an absolute goose).

'Ahah!' shrieked the nurse. 'I was completely right. There it is, on that side *there*!' In fact she was just about to poke and prod with her fat sausage fingers, and fingernails like waterslides . . . when suddenly the phone rang again.

She left the room to answer it and as soon as she'd waddled out the door Zeke took Eppie from his right-hand pocket and tucked her down his shirt. Then, with a noise like rumbling thunder, the nurse rolled back into the room.

'Now, where were we?' she said as she wobbled in closer. 'Show me your right-hand side.'

She looked for the lump on the right-hand side but it had miraculously disappeared. So finally Zeke said, 'See, there's nothing there. Please can I go out and play?'

'No you may not!' the nurse roared. 'I know it's here somewhere. I've seen it twice, and it's obviously dangerous because it's wandering all over your body.'

She checked Zeke's legs and his arms and his ears and his head and his back, and finally checked under his shirt in case the lump was on his tummy.

'Oh my gosh, there it is!' she cried. 'It's

absolutely enormous! I think we'll have to operate!'

And then the phone rang yet again and Nurse left the room once more.

Zeke stood there with Eppie curled up like a snail deep down inside his shirt.

'Operate!' gasped Zeke.

'Operate!' gasped Eppie.

'Blood and guts and pain and gore!' they gasped (at exactly the same time) and then they both just fainted.

They fell to the floor with a crash and a bang, knocking over this and bashing over that and spilling absolutely everything in sight.

When they came to, Zeke whispered loudly, 'You realise this is all your fault!' and Eppie said, 'No, it's yours.'

Then the nurse came back into the room to see a boy on the floor with no bumps at all talking to a tiny little girl with a yo-yo on her head.

'Aaaaa-a-a-a-aaaaaaaaaagh!' shrieked the nurse.

With a huff and a puff she rang the ambulance and wheezed rather urgently down the phone, 'Come quickly, come quickly! Come and get me! I've gone quite mad. I'm seeing things!'

(And the ambulance came and tried to take her to hospital but she was so fat she got stuck in the doorway and that, by the way, is where she is right now.)

Zeke and Eppie couldn't simply walk out the door, because it was blocked by a big fat nurse, so they had to find another way out.

So with no choices left, Zeke put
Eppie back in his pocket and went to
climb out the window. Easy. No one
would spot him. He'd just jump straight
out and be free. Except for one teensy
weensy problem: it was a lot further
down than he'd imagined.

So he stood on the windowsill
thinking of a plan. Thinking, thinking,
thinking, thinking. You could hear
Zeke's brain creaking and groaning and
straining, until a little voice inside his
pocket squeaked, 'Grab the branch and
swing to that tree trunk, and then we
can slide down to the ground.'

'Oh – easy for *you* to say,' Zeke said rudely, but out of habit more than intentional impoliteness. Then he stood up straight and hurled himself forward, grabbed a branch of the nearby tree, and swung with all his might to reach the trunk. Everything was going well until he accidentally swung too close to another branch, and his shorts were snagged, pulled right down and off!

Well, there was Zeke in the tree, in his embarrassing Barbie doll undies. (It's a long story, too long to go into, but I think the lesson we can all learn from the Barbie doll undies incident is never to let your mother go shopping without her glasses.)

A cool breeze whistled as he watched his shorts swinging there, stuck out of reach on a branch back near the windowsill.

'Oh no, don't let me get caught now!' he moaned as Eppie called out loudly from

way over in the pocket of his dangling
shorts, 'Hey, Mr Fancy Pants, come back
across and get me.'

Now if Zeke had had the choice he
would have left Eppie hanging there from
that branch for ever, until mice started to
live in her ears and her hair turned into
creeping vines full of thorns and
poisonous roses.

But he had to get his shorts because
he had to get his yo-yo (which he
loved), and his yo-yo was attached to
Eppie's hair, so most unfortunately he
had to get Eppie as well.

So using the same branch that had
got him to the tree trunk Zeke tried to
swing back to the window ledge . . .
but the branch snapped in half and
plummeted to the ground.

'I'm waiting, Mr Frilly Knicks,' Eppie
called out.

Zeke thought of jumping back to the window, sticking a sock in Eppie's mouth and then joining a Barbie-undies-wearing-yo-yoless monastery, but then he spotted the long green hose that was used to water the school garden. He reached over and down with his left hand, while he clung to the tree with his right, and he tried to grab the garden hose, but he missed it by just the tips of his fingers. (This was actually the one moment in all his life that he wished he was Captain Hook, or even a Transformer who could change himself into a massive fighter jet with claws that could hover over his shorts, take Eppie out of the pocket, drop her into a man-eating spider's web, and then bring the shorts back safe and sound ready to be worn back into class.)

Nup. He couldn't reach the hose with his hands, so he tried to reach it with his feet. He tried his right foot first, and yes he could just touch the hose. But there was no way that he could pick it up. So he tried his left foot. Now luckily Zeke had a remarkably long big toe on the end of that foot, so he took off his left shoe and dangled his left foot down near the hose, and before you know it he'd scooped up the hose with his big, big toe and was ready to loop the hose over a branch and swing like Tarzan all the way back to the window ledge.

And that's what he did. He swung to the windowsill, picked up his shorts, put them back on (with Eppie still in the pocket) and then swung as hard as he could, hanging from the hose, through the air to get back to the big tree trunk. All was looking beeee-you-ti-ful when suddenly someone turned the hose on and completely soaked Eppie and Zeke.

And they landed on the tree trunk

just as the bell rang for the end of recess, and all the kids went into class – except for Zeke and Eppie because they were both as sopping wet as facecloths soaking in a big cold bath.

Zeke sat waiting in the tree until all the other kids had disappeared, then he climbed carefully down the trunk to the ground, took Eppie and the yo-yo out of his pocket and tried to get them all dry.

He stood in the sun and he stood in the breeze, but the drying was taking for ever. So finally Zeke started to run, to make his own breeze and make himself hotter, and hopefully dry them faster. He started to run slowly, just round in a circle, with Eppie still tight in his hand, but then he got bored (of course) and he let the yo-yo string unwind, and ran faster and faster with Eppie dangling on the end. It was great fun and they were squealing with joy, going faster and faster, but when they were all completely dry they stopped to discover that now, it wasn't just Eppie's hair that was tangled, but Eppie herself was tied in a knot!

'Wow, bummer,' groaned Zeke.

He went back to class and sat down just as the lesson was starting. Then he quietly took the whole knotty mess out of his pocket and tried to undo Eppie under his desk. But as he fumbled and mumbled he pretty soon realised that she was actually in a super bad knot with her hands tied behind her back and her legs crossed with her feet up her nose.

Zeke tried to slip the string just once over Eppie's head. He tried to slip her arms around the string and tip her upside down very fast, and he tried turning her like a corkscrew while he counted to one hundred and sang *Row Row Row Your Boat* while breathing in. He also tried to lift her legs round her head and behind her back and between her fingers and under her nose and through one ear and out the other side – but that didn't seem to work either.

So finally Zeke said, 'This is all your fault. You just aren't trying at all.'

'I am so!' Eppie answered angrily.

'You are not,' said Zeke. 'You're just sitting there, happy as can be, while I do all the work.'

'Am not,' said Eppie.

'Are so,' said Zeke.

'Am not.'

'Are so.'

'Am not.'

'Are so.'

'Am not,' said Eppie, getting louder and louder.

'Are so!' said Zeke as loud as the horn on a ship in the middle of a foggy night. 'Are so, are so, are so. You're a selfish, lazy spoilt brat. You're a bum, you're a bum, you're a bum.'

'I beg your pardon, Zeke,' said Miss Snailheadface, who thought Zeke was talking to her.

'Um, nothing,' said Zeke.

'No: I heard you say something, and I think you said that I was a bum, a bum, a bum.'

'No,' said Zeke. 'What I said was: "I love my school, I'm as happy as Santa, ho hum, ho hum, ho hum".'

'I see,' she replied, 'and what's that in your hand?'

'Um . . . it's my yo-yo, Miss Snailheadface.'

'A yo-yo!' she said, 'A yo-yo in my class! Do you think my classroom is a circus?'

'No,' Zeke replied, 'I don't think it's a circus.' But he thought it was a good idea.

'Well you can't have that thing here in my classroom. I'm confiscating your yo-yo, from this moment on. Zeke, come here and give it to me.'

She held out her hand and waited for the yo-yo, but Zeke was too scared to move. He stood perfectly still . . . and the clock ticked loudly.

Meanwhile, skinny Miss Snailheadface (who was probably a witch) was still waiting with her long, skinny hand stretched out.

And she said in her high, scratchy, squeaky voice, 'Well? Zeke, give it to me.'

Zeke thought of a million excuses, a million lies, a million things that he wished would happen right there and then, like being stolen by a robber and traded for gold, or turning into a piece of dust and blowing out the window, or suddenly becoming evil green slime and sliding himself through the cracks in the floor, underneath the classroom, where he could live happily just eating flies and never having to tidy his room, ever.

Zeke thought and he thought, and he tried and he tried, he wished and he wished, with his eyes squished tight. But he just stayed the same old Zeke, with his sister and his yo-yo held tightly in his hand.

More seconds tick-tocked by.

Slowly Zeke moved his hand forward towards scarecrow skinny Miss Snailheadface. Zeke was scared, and Eppie was scared, and they both knew now they would definitely get busted and their parents would find out, and they'd never get pocket money ever again for the rest of their lives, and never get to eat pizza or chips or burgers on Friday night, and probably be sent to their rooms for at least two years, and when they were finally released they would walk outside and see that the whole world was filled with strange creatures from outer space and amazing cars, and super cool technology, and actually getting busted was starting to sound all right . . .

Anyway, Zeke was scared, and Eppie was scared, but of course there was no choice and Zeke had to give the yo-yo to Miss Snailheadface. So he held out his hand and put the yo-yo and the tangled string and his knotted tiny little sister into Miss Snailheadface's skinny stick-fingers.

Miss Snailheadface didn't look down. She just smiled like a shark straight into Zeke's eyes and said, 'There now: that wasn't so hard.'

'But what will you do with my yo-yo?' Zeke asked.

'Oh,' said Miss Snailheadface. 'This bit of rubbish? I'll take it up to the principal's office and she will either put it in her bottom drawer and leave it there for ever or else she will send it in an envelope to Africa where it will probably get eaten by a large green snake.'

'Oh great,' thought Eppie, 'that's just what I need.' (Panic, panic, panic.)

Then Eppie (who was pretty smart) made a squeak just like a hungry mouse

and Miss Snailheadface
screeeeeeeeeeeeeeeeeeeeeeeeeeeeeeeamed,
jumped up onto the desk and dropped
Eppie and the yo-yo and the tangled
string right into the bin.

'There, that's that!' said Miss Snailheadface (after her teeth had stopped nattering in fear).

So Zeke sat down, back at his desk, and Eppie sat in the bin, and the lessons returned to normal (except that Miss Snailheadface was still standing on the desk and Dimitri Wilson was trying to look up her dress).

After a while Darryn Pinky got up from his desk and put his leaking texta in the bin, on top of Eppie. Then Claire Blump emptied her pencil sharpener in the bin, Eleanor Tonsil put her ruined wet painting in the bin, Tim Sneak put Erica's plait in the bin, and Jake Rat cleared out the whole back of his desk and put an old orange, a smelly banana and a piece of melted chocolate all in the bin, right on top of Eppie.

Then the bell rang for lunch and Miss Snailheadface told goody-goody Richie

Nosesniffle and revolting Emily Pong to
go and empty the classroom bin into
the great big square metal garbage
dump at the very bottom of the school
playground.

So, of course when all the other kids went to play, Zeke, who really wanted his yo-yo back, had no choice at all but to follow goody-goody Richie Nosesniffle and revolting Emily Pong all the way to the bottom of the playground.

Zeke had to be careful that Richie Nosesniffle and Emily Pong didn't see him because they were both dreadful

sneaks and they would definitely tell
their skinny-as-a-stick teacher that
naughty Zeke had followed them down
to the big square metal garbage dump at
the bottom of the garden to steal back
his stupid yo-yo. Pathetic and um-ah.
(I mean there are worse things in the
world, like starvation and racism and war.)

So that he would not be seen, Zeke
grabbed a big leafy branch that was
taller and wider than he was. Then he hid
behind it and followed Nosesniffle and
Pong down to the dump. His disguise was
so good that no one could tell he was
Zeke at all, and he just looked like a
normal tree wearing sneakers and
running across the playground.

Finally Nosesniffle and Pong reached
the dump, and they picked up the
classroom bin and emptied out all the
rubbish. Zeke the Tree waited patiently
for the two of them to leave, but they

both just stood there and talked and talked (probably about how fabulous they were). Zeke waited and waited and waited and then, when Nosesniffle and Pong had finally walked halfway back up the playground, Zeke ran as fast as he possibly could towards the garbage, and dived into the dump.

It was really smelly inside the dump bin and it was overflowing with old sandwiches, orange peel, apple cores, plastic bags, an old shoe, a lost sock, lots

of paper, lolly wrappers, crisp packets,
drink containers and all the grass and
leaves and twigs and bugs from the
school lawn mower. Zeke searched and
searched for his yo-yo but it was
nowhere to be found. Finally he called
out: 'Eppie, where are you?'

'I'm not here.'

'I know you are,' said Zeke. 'Come on. I'm looking for my yo-yo.'

'I know that's what you're looking for,' said Eppie, 'and I know that you don't care about me one single bit! I've been up a tree, under a blow drier, soaked by a hose, stuffed in a pocket, poked and prodded, confiscated, thrown out, pinched, tickled and told to shut up. So why should I help you?'

'Because,' said Zeke in an ever increasing font size, 'if you don't tell me where my yo-yo is you'll be stuck here till you rot and smell. Because you seem to have forgotten something and

that is that I
am the only
one who
knows you're
here! And
that means
I'm the
only

one
who can
ever, ever
get you
out, and
I'll only
get you

out if
I get
my
yo-yo,
so
tell

me
where
it
is!'

Eppie sighed like a deflating balloon and said quietly, 'Your yo-yo and I are inside a milk carton, just near the eggshells, the old fish tank, the wet newspaper and half a barbecued chicken.'

Zeke followed Eppie's instructions as carefully as he could. He burrowed with his hand past the mouldy barbecued chicken and the wet newspaper and the old fish tank and the eggshells and then into the smelly milk carton where he finally found Eppie and his yo-yo.

'Yay,' he said. 'At last we can get out of here!' But then just as he was about to climb out of the bin, carrying the yo-yo and the knotted string and knotted Eppie, Zeke heard a rolling and rumbling from far away, which unfortunately was getting closer.

'Quick, duck down!' he whispered just in time, as a huge garbage truck picked up the dump and all the rubbish, and of course picked up Eppie and the yo-yo and Zeke as well. Up high went its great big metal arm, then down went the whole load into the back of the truck.

The back of the truck was filled with
a scary scraping and rattling sound.
When Zeke and Eppie were finally
brave enough to open their eyes and see
what was happening, they realised, with

a terrible shock, that the horrible noise
was an enormous rubbish shredder that
was inside the garbage truck! They were
both going to be eaten alive unless some
sort of magic spell came and saved them
just in time.

Now it's funny that Zeke and Eppie should have thought that (the bit about the magic spell) because just then, inside the garbage truck, something landed 'plonk' right in front of them. It wasn't a dead fish, or an old bike tyre or even a half-eaten meat pie. It was in fact a magic wish-making lamp, which of course was just what they were needing.

'Cool,' said Eppie and Zeke.

Quickly Zeke rubbed the lamp and before you knew it he'd wished that he and Eppie were out of the garbage truck. (Unfortunately he forgot to mention that he wanted the lamp to be out of the garbage truck with him so that he could make wish after wish after wish after wish and make himself rich and powerful and the leader of the universe.) So the magic lamp stayed in the garbage truck and was finally rediscovered in a dump by an old man in a floral suit who uses it to this very day to house his toenail clippings.

Anyway, the whole point is that Zeke and strawberry-sized Eppie had their wish come true and were magically spat out the back of the garbage truck. First Eppie and the yo-yo tumbled out of the truck and then out fell Zeke as well.

Zeke landed flat on his bum on the footpath, but Eppie flew through the air, bounced on the path and kept right on going. She and the yo-yo paused for a moment on the edge of a crack, and then ever so slowly they began to roll gently down the hill. Faster and faster and faster they rolled, down the hill, past the principal's car, past the school fence, past the big tree that gives you a rash, past the letterbox, past the corner shop, past the street corner, and smack bang like a ball at the bowling alley, into the pile of coloured glass bottles that were neatly stacked ready for recycling. Then Eppie boinged off the footpath again, over the road, under a car and way onto the other side of the black tarmac road.

By now Eppie's hair was filled with sticks and twigs and she had two pebbles stuck in her ears, but still she rolled on and on. Past the haunted house where the noisy budgie lived and

past Sam Stench's house and past
Arlette Button's house and past Igor
Watson's mum, who was standing in
their front yard spying on her
neighbours, and down and down and
down the hill. Eppie just missed the man
who was trimming the lawn with the
loud and angry lawn mower, and she
just missed a big blob of dog poo.

Meanwhile Zeke huffed and puffed in hot pursuit hoping Eppie would finally slow down. But no sooner had she crossed the black bumpy road and landed with a plompf on the grass verge, than a boy with a bike rode right over the top of her and she and the string and the yo-yo too all got caught up in the spokes.

So off she went again, only much faster this time, and the boy on the bike didn't know she was there as he rode up a hill and round a bend and imagined he was a speeding train. And Eppie was just stuck there in the spokes, whirling and whirring round and round, wishing that the stupid boy on the bike would suddenly shatter into a thousand pieces, sell himself as a puzzle and then give all the money to her so she could buy a fizzy drink, a packet of crisps and some bubblegum.

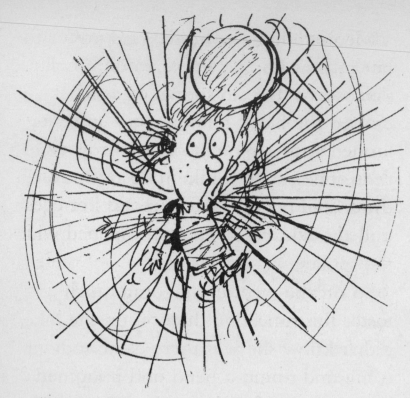

Yum.

But wait!

You see, up until that moment Eppie had been feeling OK, even though she was whirling and turning and flying round like a mouse on a great big big-dipper, but when she started to think of the milkbar and the crisps and the drink and the bubblegum, and the chocolate and ice cream and popcorn and lollies, she started to feel a bit queasy. At first it was just an idea of sickness, but then it was a giddy feeling in her head, and then in her arms and legs and toes, and finally in her stomach. And Eppie's nose squished and her eyes rolled back and her mouth opened wide and suddenly she threw up, right there and then, in a projectile vomit so big it nearly covered the universe.

The boy on the bike stopped with a screech as the lime-green vomit covered him completely, from his sneakers to the tips of his hair.

(Now although this was absolutely gross, there was a positive side to the situation because the boy's eyes were also covered in vomit so he couldn't see a thing. This gave mighty Zeke his chance to run up to the bike and remove his yo-yo and Eppie from the spokes without either of them being seen.)

And that's what he did. He rescued his yo-yo (and his sister) and looked forward to life getting back to normal. He had a grin all over his face, and his eyes twinkled and his cheeks were rosy and he was so happy he threw the tangle of Eppie and the yo-yo up into the air with a happy happy whoop – and a crow that just happened to be flying past caught them both in its beak and flew back towards the school.

So Zeke ran again, chasing them all, and arrived back at school just in time to see the bird hover over the swings and carelessly drop Eppie and the yo-yo onto the slippery dip.

They rolled down with a rush and, when they got to the bottom, they bumped into big Max Squish, who was blocking the slippery dip, and careered off the slippery dip and onto the see-saw. They rested there for a moment until Mary McNose decided to bounce with her bum on the other end of the see-saw and then with a sudden whoosh and zoosh, Eppie and the yo-yo hurtled into the air once more, right on over the playground fence and over the tennis court where Eric Birdbrain was having a tennis lesson.

Eric saw Eppie and the yo-yo coming towards his head and thought they were a tennis ball, so he got his racquet and

swung it back and hit Eppie and the
yo-yo as hard as he could with the best
forehand shot he'd ever done.

Eppie and the yo-yo flew higher and
higher and higher and higher, back over
the fence and past the school and over
the wide black road one more time. They
hit an overhead telegraph wire and fell
down from the sky and in through the
sunroof of a passing fast red sports car.

'Plop' they landed in the back seat
where a small fluffy white dog gave

them both the most enormous sticky licks as they drove on to the park. Then when the sports car stopped at the park, the fluffy white dog grabbed Eppie and the yo-yo in his teeth and leapt through the car window.

The blonde lady who had been driving the car got out as well, looked bug-eyed at her yappy fluffy dog and said in a high little voice that sounded like she was being squeezed, 'Oh my little sugar-poopsie-woopsie-doopsie-schnoops, what have you got there?'

And of course the dog didn't answer

(for a thousand reasons, too many to mention).

'Give it to me,' the blonde woman said as she stood there in her ridiculously tight T-shirt and unnecessarily short skirt. 'Give it to me and we'll play catch.' Then she picked up Eppie and the yo-yo in her suntanned hand with her long purple fingernails and without looking carefully or even thinking for one moment threw Eppie and the yo-yo as far as she could across the big wide park, where they landed smack-bang in a huge muddy puddle.

Of course the small white dog and the suntanned blonde woman didn't want to get grubby (not when looking crisp, blonde and groomed was really the only thing either had going for them) so they left Eppie and the yo-yo in the mud.

Now Zeke, puffing like a sick kettle and sweating like cheese in the sun, saw Eppie and the yo-yo lying there, and he crawled up to them exhausted. He picked up his yo-yo and gave it a kiss (making sure he didn't kiss his tangled sister, because then he'd get germs and his lips would fall off and well, you know – the usual), and he said, 'Oh my darling yo-yo, it's so good to hold you again.' (Yes, I know what you're thinking, but that actually is what he said.)

Happy, Zeke started to walk back to school. He was completely content and grinning wildly at his yo-yo and thinking of all the good times to come when suddenly a big booming voice from behind said, 'Hey you, I think I'll have that.'

It was Buster Wallace, the class bully. 'I'll close my eyes and count to three,' he said. 'Then you can put that yo-yo in my cap and we'll all pretend nothing ever happened.'

Now, Zeke had been scared of his
mother and the teacher and the big fat
nurse and of course the lime-green vomit,
but nothing in the world scared him as
much as Buster because, like all bullies,
Buster Wallace was incredibly stupid and
you couldn't explain a thing to him. (And
bullies tend to hurt people when they don't
get what they want.)

So Buster closed his eyes and counted to
three and Zeke put Eppie and the yo-yo in
Buster's baseball cap. Then Buster put his
cap on his head and ran back to school.
Zeke chased him as fast as he could, but
just when they got inside the gate, the bell
rang for them to go into class.

Sitting at his desk, Zeke was terrified.
'Please could I have my yo-yo?' he
whispered to Buster.

'No.'

'Please, I'll give you my swap cards,'
said Zeke.

'And?' said Buster.

'And my favourite book.'

'And?'

'And my football.'

'And?'

'And my cricket bat, and brand new watch and my favourite shoes that glow in the dark.'

'And?' said Buster, enjoying himself immensely as he watched Zeke squirm.

'You know I really want to give you your yo-yo, but it'll take more than anything you've offered so far.'

'I'll do your homework for the rest of your life.'

'Yes, and what else?' Buster raised his eyebrows.

But Zeke couldn't think of anything else, so he sat there yo-yoless and Eppie stayed with smelly stupid Buster and sobbed quietly in his cap.

Zeke heard Eppie sob and he felt sorry for her.

But he felt more sorry for himself.

Not only was he without a yo-yo but their mum was going to kill him.

I mean, it's all very well to spend every single day of your life wishing your sister would get eaten by cannibals, but the reality is – well – well, the reality is that he sort of love— oops, forget I ever said that, no he sort of liked – well no, he didn't like her, he – he—

Well the reality is that their mum was going to kill him if he didn't get his sister back.

'I might give it to you at midnight tonight. That is, if you're good,' teased Buster. 'I'll meet you in the cemetery by the old crook's grave, and you can give me everything you own, and I'll give you your stupid yo-yo.'

Zeke was scared to death, but he said, 'No, I need it right now.'

'Well, make an offer,' Buster grinned.

'I can't, I've got nothing left.'

And then Zeke began crying softly at his desk, but he pretended he just had a cold.

For the first time in his entire life Zeke's afternoon passed too quickly. Zeke's mum would be here to collect them soon and there was no way he could try to pretend that Eppie had just gone to the toilet – not for the rest of her life.

'Oh no,' he whimpered.

Then finally, late in the afternoon when the going home bell was about to ring, Zeke popped up with a brilliant idea. 'I take back everything that I've offered so far,' he said to Buster in a strangely strong and sure voice. 'I have something heaps better. I'll give you . . . I'll give you . . . I'll . . . I'll . . . I'll give you . . . I'll give you my father's private jet with its own computer games, swimming pool, motorbike, yo-yo and racing car! But I can't give it to you until tomorrow. Is that OK with you?'

Buster paused for a moment, not wanting to look too keen, then he said very slowly, 'OK, it's a deal. I'll give you the yo-yo now and get all those other things from you tomorrow.'

Under his breath Zeke said to himself, 'Wow, lucky he's as thick as a brick, 'cause I thought everybody everywhere knew that tomorrow never comes.'

So just as the bell went Buster gave
the yo-yo back to Zeke, complete with
tiny little Eppie, who was so tangled up
she was invisible amongst the string.
Then Zeke packed up his things and
left the classroom at the end of a very,
very, very long day. He walked to the
playground to wait for their mum,
stand under a tree, and untangle Eppie.

This leg through that loop and up round the ear.

He was extremely patient as he slowly unknotted her. He was feeling really good and exceptionally kind. In fact, when he'd finished untangling her he was going to stretch her back to her original size (if not a little bit bigger), and be nice to her for the rest of her life. He was. But before he did that Zeke said to Eppie, as she still hung from the yo-yo by her hair, 'I'm sorry, Eppie; it's been a tough day. Want to go for a ride before Mum comes?'

And Eppie, of course, said, 'Yes.'

So Zeke unwound his yo-yo, with Eppie attached, and started to run through some basic tricks. First he did that simple up and down spinning trick and Eppie began to giggle. Then he Walked the Dog, and Rocked the Cradle, and did The Elevator and Bite Your Bum.

And then he did Sleep Walker
and Eiffel Tower
and Cats' Whiskers
and Eppie was laughing and laughing.

And finally, with great delight, just as Mum came round the corner, Zeke said, 'Hold on tight and close your eyes I'm going to do Round the World!'

So Eppie held on tight, and closed her eyes, and Zeke swung that string out as far as he could, and it was the greatest beginning to Round the World that had actually ever been seen. He could have won the Olympic Games of beginnings to yo-yo tricks.

But just when Eppie and the yo-yo got their speed up and were way out there on the string, the string broke, and Eppie flew off, and she went off round the world by herself (with the yo-yo and the string still attached to her hair).

Right round the world.

Silently Zeke watched Eppie
disappear with her arms waving madly
and her mouth yelling,
'aaaaaaaaaaaaaaaaaaaaagh,'

past the trees,

past the skyscrapers,

past the clouds and the planes and the helicopters and satellites, past the sun.

And she was just passing the moon (ready to zoom over the Arctic) when Zeke heard his mum honk from the car, and he mumbled to himself, alone in the playground, 'Gee, Eppie has all the fun!'

About the author, Gretel Killeen;

Gretel Killeen started writing comedy by accident when she stood up to perform a very serious poem and everybody laughed.

From here she moved to writing and performing comedy in a variety of theatres and clubs across her home country, Australia, and for a number of major radio stations. Gretel's comedy writing then led to television and in 2001 Gretel hosted Australia's *Big Brother* – a phenomenal success which she repeated in 2002.

Gretel has published a number of best-selling books that will split your sides and make your head explode. After you read them, you'll never be the same again.

She lives in Sydney's famous Bondi with her two children, Zeke and Eppie – the stars of *My Sister's a Yo-yo* and *My Sister's an Alien*.

GRETEL KILLEEN

My Sister's an Alien

When Eppie gets **squished** to the size of a **strawberry**, ends up **flying** round the world, landing on planet sock and about to be kidnapped by a **handsome alien** prince, it's up to her brother Zeke to rescue her. What follows is a **laugh-a-minute** adventure full of short-sighted cats, space rockets, **burps**, possums, owls, **goodies**, **baddies**, galactic battles, **movie stars**, superstars, false **moustaches**, girls' nighties, flying horses, footballs, diamonds and **lovesick Martians** – and that's all before Mum wakes up.

'Madly inventive and very funny'
JACQUELINE WILSON

0099433672
£3.99